Published by: Smackachunk! Creative Studio AB
www.smackachunk.com

Sandwich Expedition! 1890 - A Penny and Polo Adventure

Written by: Ken Cursoe & Ann Halvorsen
Written and Illustrated by: Jay Sopp

Special tally-hos to:

Ken Cursoe
The very cool Kevin, Lori, Maddie & Lottie Franck
Ed & Lynn Hidek
Henry Carter Hull Library (Clinton, CT)
Penguins and polar bears everywhere

Penny and Polo created by: Jay Sopp

First Smackachunk Creative Studio AB edition, 2006
ISBN 91-631-8133-9 (pre-2007 ISBN)
ISBN 978-91-631-8133-7 (post-2006 ISBN)

Lovingly printed in Sweden (you've never been?) by:
Kristianstad Boktryckeri AB
Kristianstad, 2006

Please draw in the rest of this space.

Sandwich Expedition!
1890

A Penny & Polo Adventure!

{Fig. 1 Expeditionary Accoutrements}

Hello Fellow Adventurer:

Pennington P. Pennyworth here. I say, your signing on for one of our thrilling expeditions leaves me quite chuffed!

The legacy of the Pennyworth and Polo families stems from a long line of avid adventurers. Let's see, there was Major Penny P. Pennyworth and his fearless expeditions into the jungles of Sumatra. Then there were the infamous Yeti Observation Campaigns in the Himalayas by Sir Penny D. Pennyworth. Ah, and let's not forget Penny C. Pennyworth, Esq. and his relentless exploration of the social order of the East Hamptons. All done with Polos by their side and all well-documented. Indeed, the Pennyworths are made from the right stuff.

Now, where did I put that muffin? I say, all this typing leaves me positively famished. Ah, food, that reminds me of one particularly daring expedition embarked upon by my inspiring forefather Pendleton G. Pennyworth and his ever-present adventure partner Polo. The expedition in question took place in the late 1800s and involves a true global trek in the name of royal gastronomy and national pride.

{Fig. 2 Pendleton's Patented Pen}

Naturally, it starts off at the famous address of 221A Baker Street in London. As historians, scholars and adventurers are all aware; this was once the home of the Slightest Inkling Society of Exploration. It is from that destination we begin! And it is from there the writings of Pendleton G. Pennyworth and Polo start.

So, dive into the historic journals of my forefathers, strap on your explorer boots and make sure to bring your best binoculars. We're off.

Tally Ho!

Pennington P. Pennyworth, Penguin and Inkling

Penny burst into the den of the Slightest Inkling Society with his usual enthusiasm and excitement, madly waving an open envelope and letter - not giving a care in the world as to who might get a paper cut. It is with this particular brand of reckless abandon that P.G. Pennyworth entered all adventures - and rooms, come to think of it.

"Look, Polo! We have received a letter from the Palace of the Queen! Oh, my, this is serious. Seems like national honor is at stake. The Queen writes that the Americans have invented something called a 'hamburger.' Apparently it is all the rage." Penny continued his reading with great care. "Ah, this is where it gets interesting. The Queen is commissioning us to come up with a spectacular sandwich that will rival this so-called 'hamburger' and put our country back on the culinary map."

Penny could hardly contain his excitement. His mouth actually began watering just thinking about future knighting ceremonies and accolades. These types of rewards were of course to be expected for anyone who could successfully resolve such a national crisis.

"There might be a medal for us in this, old boy," Penny said in a positively pleased manner as he turned to his trusted friend and fellow explorer, Polo. "We'll have to pull out all the stops on this one, Polo."

{Fig. 3 Lickable Royalty of 1890 - commonly known as a stamp}

Penny waddled over to one of the many bookcases that lined the walls of the Slightest Inkling and removed an old scroll from one of the shelves. He blew off the dust and carefully unrolled the ancient sheet of paper. Polo studied the scroll with a critical eye. This particular polar bear was never one to rush into adventures without a proper risk-benefit analysis and at this early stage he was far from convinced.

"This, my dear furry friend," Penny said confidently, "is the lost recipe of Montagu, the inventor of the sandwich and a dear friend of my great-great-great grandfather. Montagu said it would be the most delicious thing ever put between two slices of bread. We are the only ones with this recipe and with it we will create the decisive sandwich. Ha, hamburger, you don't stand a chance."

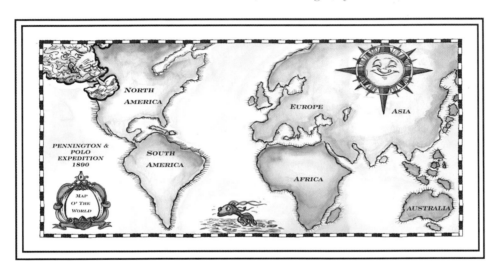

Penny went over to the globe located in the corner of the room and looked at it very carefully. Geography was a passion shared by all members of the Slightest Inkling Society and the globe in question bore all the signs of the numerous well-planned adventures that generations of Inklings had taken part in. Well, some adventures were more planned than others. Come to think of it, there was rarely any planning involved at all. The globe's wear and tear was actually the result of an abundance of impromptu football games and buoyancy experiments. "It will be a difficult sandwich to make. The ingredients are scattered all over the world." Penny had entered his contemplative state, but it passed quickly — as it usually did. "But we must do this for Queen and Country," he continued quite assertively. "Let us be off, old chap. Adventure awaits!"

And with that, Penny and Polo packed their bags and set off on their worldwide expedition to peacefully resolve this culinary crisis. You might even call it the Hamburger Crisis of 1890.

FEBRUARY 2, PARIS, FRANCE:

Polo and I have begun our search for the ingredients to the ultimate sandwich. The recipe calls for a special kind of bread from France called a baguette. We have tried asking the natives where this bread can be found, but unfortunately no one here speaks the Queen's English. However, Polo has pointed out a man in white makeup wearing a striped shirt performing in the park. We have high hopes that once we get him to talk he will tell us where we can find a baguette.

{Fig. 4 La baguette géante de Paris}

After almost creating an international incident involving the performing arts and a baseball bat, Penny and Polo made their way around the Mediterranean to the exciting continent of Africa. On their way, Penny picked up an outstandingly good stick, which he thought would have a particularly promising future as a tool of exploration. Indeed, you never know what you might run into in the bush and Penny had been forced to leave his much beloved baseball bat in Paris - for diplomatic reasons, you see. It was a shame really. The bat had been an authentic Boston Beaneaters bat, but that's another story entirely. Anyway, a good stick was indeed needed and Penny was happy with his choice. As the old penguin adage goes: "It is a smart waterfowl that remains at a poking distance."

FEBRUARY 6, CAIRO, EGYPT:

We are in Egypt looking for a Middle Eastern delicacy called falafel. It is a fried patty of seasoned, ground up chickpeas and from what I hear is quite delicious.

Mmm. Sounds like just the thing for this year's Christmas pudding!

{Fig. 5 Sheathed Chickpeas}

A Tasty Recipe for a Fine Falafel

1 cup of ChickPeas
1/2 Cup chopped onions
1/4 Cup Chopped Parsley
3 pressed Garlic cloves
2 Eggs

Spice it up with Coriander, Cumin, Red/Black Pepper. Mash the peas like a mad little monkey and mix all the ingredients. Shape into small flattened meatballs & fry them in some oil until golden brown. Serve in a Pita with some lettuce, tomatoes, and cucumbers.

Ripping Good Times!

CAIRO, EGYPT (CONTINUED):

I have determined that the best place to search for falafel is in one of the busy and aromatic markets in the city. Mind you, these markets tend to be quite chaotic, but I am confident that our vast exploration experience and proven methods will lead us directly to the required dish.

Our adventurers arrived at a Cairo market place where Polo began bartering with a merchant for the next ingredient. Penny kept busy putting his new poking stick into practice, inadvertently poking a hole into a twenty pound bag of cumin with disastrous results.

He later added the following entry to his journal:

 NOTE TO SELF: I may have to abandon stick-poking as a viable tool of exploration.

Penny and Polo were now ready to venture further into the exotic lands of Africa. There were after all many more ingredients to collect. They managed to join a camel caravan heading to western Africa. Penny felt particularly prepared for the pending Sahara crossing with his trusted pith helmet fastened securely on his head. Penny was in fact quite fond of hats. He often philosophically asked: "How can I be an adventurer without a hat?" A valid question, indeed.

{Fig. 6 Pith Helmet}

A must-have in every true adventurer's inventory. A pith helmet is a lightweight helmet made of cork and covered with cloth. Its main purpose is to provide the much needed cranial coolness sought after in the tropics. The pith helmet's design was partly inspired by the German pickelhaube; although sadly no pickles were included in the final design.

FEBRUARY 14, GHANA, AFRICA:

Polo and I have been searching the wilds of Africa for an ingredient called foo-foo. It can be added to soups or eaten by itself. It is made of mashed yams, which are native to this fabulous continent. The genius of Montagu lies in the foo-foo's application between two pieces of bread. Apparently, a large stick is used in the mashing process. I say, perhaps the decision to abandon my beloved poking stick was rather premature.

LESSON LEARNED: One must not be too hasty when assigning value to a stick.

We have heard that wild boars are quite the fans of yams. Exactly how these animals manage to handle the large stick required in the foo-foo making process remains a mystery. Wild boars are elusive, but I'm sure once we find one of these creatures we will also find yams and foo-foo nearby. Polo is an expert tracker so the old chap shouldn't have any trouble finding a wild boar.

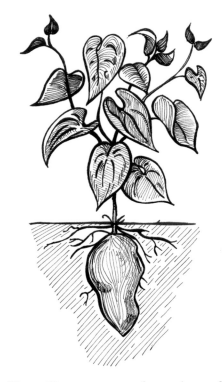

{Fig. 7 Yam - in a state of unmasheyness}

The ingredients were piling up and it was time
to turn in an eastward direction. Polo for one
was only too happy to leave his somewhat
hostile wildlife encounters of Africa behind.
He had found that penguin-inspired missions
were not always as well planned as they could
be. Polo was decidedly ready for a jungle of
the urban kind.

They decided to journey by train to their next destination. Now, you would think that this train business would be a fairly simple endeavor, but there are no simple endeavors when a penguin is involved. Penny kept insisting on jumping on random trains and guessing where they were heading by looking excitedly out of the window. Eventually, Polo convinced Penny that a more systematic approach to train-taking may have its merits, such as deciding upon a destination and looking at time tables. Less attractive, perhaps, but far more efficient. Penny's approach had its own set of merits, however, and perhaps one day someone will make a game show out of it.

{Fig. 8 Mortar & Pestle}

FEBRUARY 21, BOMBAY, INDIA:

Curry is the next ingredient on the list and we have arrived in India to find it. Quite a brilliant move on Polo's part in fact. He reminded me that a good friend of the Pennyworth family resides in India, which is known for its curry abundance. Good show! The friend has promised to meet us with a jar of the stuff.

I say, this should be an easy task. She said she would be wearing a yellow and purple sari. She really ought to stand out in a crowd with such an outfit!

The great thing about adventuring is that you always learn new stuff. One lesson learned in Bombay was that colorful saris are not as uncommon as you might think. In fact, the appointed rendezvous took a great deal longer than anticipated. Hours of searching the crowded streets of Bombay combined with Penny's less than organized approach to train-taking in Africa, forced the duo to face up to the stark reality. They were running terribly behind schedule. After some deliberation, they decided to take a short-cut over the Himalayas to their next destination, China.

Penny donned his blue Sherpa hat for the occasion. While Polo was still trying to get his head around the sheer number of hats his penguin friend was able to fit into his explorer pack, Penny had moved on to filling up his thermos with hot tea. "I say, Polo, this Darjeeling tea is simply cracking. It's just the sort of refreshment daring explorers like us need on high altitude journeys. This Indian lot sure knows how to brew a good cup of tea." Polo decided to bring an ample supply of strong rope in addition to the tea. He had a feeling it would come in handy.

{Fig. 9 Multiple Slabs of Soft and Gooshy Tofu}

FEBRUARY 28, BEIJING, CHINA:

Polo and I made it to China. Indeed, the mountain crossing was a breeze. In fact, I'm not sure what all the treacherous Mt. Everest rumors are all about. Well, we're off to find tofu. It is made of soybeans and used in all sorts of dishes, from soups to desserts. It looks like a white brick, but I am told it is rather tasty.

We are, however, in need of tofu of royal proportions, so Polo and I will search around the Great Wall of China in hopes of finding the Great Tofu of China. It shouldn't take too long; after all, how big can this wall be?

Now, as you know, Penny and Polo belong to an adventurer club back in London called the Slightest Inkling Society. The club regularly puts on calisthenics sessions for its members to ensure the needed level of fitness among explorers. Nothing, however, had prepared our adventurous duo for close to 4000 miles of bricks, hills and steps in the search of tofu. A Great Wall indeed!

Now that tofu had been secured, Penny and Polo had to bid farewell to Asia and head for South America. An ocean crossing lay ahead. "What's the name of this ocean again?" Penny asked Polo. Polo indicated that they would be tackling the Pacific Ocean. "Pacific, eh? That sounds all right. I am certainly up for a civilized and relaxing sail after our recent exertions," Penny said quite pleased. Polo was not convinced, however. He knew the Pacific Ocean quite well and was very familiar with its turbulent and fickle conditions. Polo did not anticipate a relaxing sail.

MARCH 17, THE AMAZON, BRAZIL:

We have made it to one of the least explored places on earth, the Amazon rain forest in Brazil. This jungle is full of exotic fruits that would go very nicely indeed with our sandwich, but the recipe calls for cupuaco and this mission is too important to risk straying from the given formula. We grabbed a crate-full of the stuff.

This task was a doddle so Polo and I had time to enjoy a leisurely sail. The locals told us about a fish that apparently has a bite to it. A piranha, they call it. I am a bit on the peckish side of things, so I'll have to keep a keen eye out for this flavorful fish treat.

{Fig. 10 The Decidedly Unfishlike Cupuaco}

Penny and Polo eventually made it out of the
Amazonian jungle, but not without noticing
that the river water in this hemisphere held
unusual properties. Their canoe paddles
seemed to mysteriously disintegrate as if
they were being chewed off in the river. No
wonder there were no signs of the purported
piranha. How could anything survive in
such a hostile environment? They had no
time to investigate this further, however.
They were about to enter the territory
of their culinary adversaries. Their full
attention was needed.

{Fig. 11 The Statue of Liberty - The one in New York, not Paris}

MARCH 21, NEW YORK CITY, AMERICA:

This is truly a peculiar place. The natives speak of a rather Big Apple, but Polo and I have only spotted apples of quite the ordinary sort. It certainly makes you wonder how a people so confused about foodstuffs can invent something like the "hamburger."

We need to put the produce problem aside, however, as we are searching for something called a "hot dog." It sounds like quite a frightful dish and I may have to step in and deal with this less than civilized situation.

Apparently, hot dogs are being sold by a large number of street vendors. If this is true, we will soon be heading back home to present Her Majesty with Montagu's brilliant sandwich.

Now, the Pennyworth family is well-known for its ability to leap to wild conclusions in a single bound. Pendleton G. Pennyworth was no exception. The word "hot" triggered a completely logical jump from food to a high-pressure fire hose in Penny's nimble mind. The details of the incident in question have unfortunately been lost to time and wet journal pages. The only surviving entry is this short journal post script:

PS: The so-called "dogs" were not as hot as anticipated.

Transatlantic travel can take many forms. For instance, the first transatlantic radio message was sent from Poldhu in England to Signal Hill in Canada on December 12, 1901. On the receiving end stood an excited Guglielmo Marconi propping up the needed reception antenna with a high flying kite. On that cold winter's day in 1901 his hard work paid off as he received the first spine-tingling message from across the ocean. It read: "S."

{Fig. 12 The S.S. Ess}

The journey back across the Atlantic Ocean on board the S.S. Ess was only marginally smoother than the trip across the Pacific Ocean. The waves and weather had only subsided when they pulled into London. Could the voyage have been an omen for things to come? Did they carry in their possession a means to answer the Hamburger Conundrum? Time was indeed of the essence!

Penny and Polo returned to 221A Baker Street with all their ingredients where they carefully followed the recipe and assembled the sandwich. It took three horse-drawn carriages and twenty strong penguins to carry Montagu's monstrous meal through the narrow streets and passages. The procession quickly made its way to the Royal Palace.

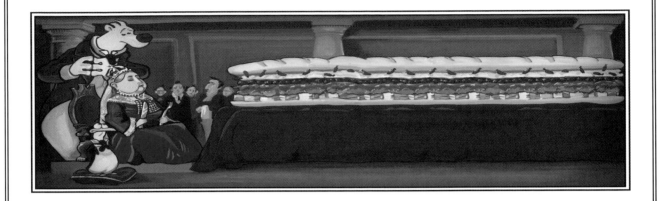

When they arrived at the palace the carriages and accompanying penguins returned to Baker Street. This left P.G. and Polo to face Her Majesty and the royal court alone. Although the pair had faced many harrowing experiences in the past, the tension they were feeling at this moment seemed to surpass any felt before. It was indeed a privilege to meet the Queen under ordinary circumstances, but today was no ordinary day. Today was the day they would present their answer to the Hamburger question.

With the Hamburger threat looming on the shores of Britain, they were here to save the nation's culinary honor. This was a heavy weight to be placed upon the shoulders of a polar bear and a penguin. They bowed to the Queen and court and removed the silk drape that lavishly covered their creation. The entire court eyed Montagu's long-lost sandwich; the sandwich of all sandwiches. She delicately tucked in her royal napkin and picked up her royal silverware.

The Queen took a single bite of the sandwich. She chewed it slowly and thoughtfully. Her advisors watched anxiously, but were too afraid to speak. Our explorer twosome watched nervously.

It was during her last three or four chomps that P. G. Pennyworth and Polo came upon a single and startling thought. To their horror, the two realized that neither of them had actually sampled the sandwich before giving it to the Queen. They had no idea what the blasted thing tasted like. Oh dear, oh dear, oh dear!

The Queen put the sandwich down and swallowed the morsel. She gently placed her fork and knife on the table in front of her and cleared her throat. She was now going to address the explorers. This was the stuff great historical moments were made of!

"Mister Pennyworth and Mister Polo, this sandwich is truly the most unusual and strangest tasting thing I've ever had."

Penny and Polo both gasped. The advisors and royal court gasped. She had addressed the sandwich as "thing". What could it mean?!? Advisors began to panic! The royal court began to panic. Rumors spread! People fainted in the street as chickens started to remove their own feathers. Newts were observed swimming backwards in village ponds across the country!

Penny and Polo froze and fully expected the next words from the Queen's mouth to be:

"Throw these two in the dungeon and make them eat every last bit of this ghastly sandwich!"

Polo envisioned years of slowly wasting away in a dark and damp prison cell; locked away until they had finished eating the ghastly sandwich. And to top it all off - torture; oh yes, there would undoubtedly be torture. Penny pondered what, if anything, he could write in his journal:

TOWER OF LONDON, ENGLAND:

Date unknown, sandwich still here.

The situation did appear bleak. Oh dear, oh dear, oh dear! What more could be said?

But instead the Queen left the dining table, walked out onto the balcony and addressed the crowd waiting below.

"Because this is one of the most unique and flavorful things I have ever eaten, I am honored to declare your mission successfully completed."

Oh, jubilation! Penny and Polo let out a sigh of relief. The Queen presented them with their royal laurels for successfully answering the nation's call for help during a period filled with hamburger uncertainties.

Penny couldn't wait to get back to his colleagues at the Slightest Inkling Society. There were so many stories to tell and there was of course the matter of the shiny - the very, very, oh so delightfully shiny – medal that hung gloatingly around his neck. It needed to be shown off! Polo was also eager to get back to the club. He was certainly due some strong tea and serious newspaper reading after all the mountain climbing, boar chasing and ocean sailing he had been through recently.

Polo soon settled into his favorite chair and rolled his eyes as he overhead Penny in the other room. His penguin partner was already excitedly entertaining Inklings with stories about his run-in with the French authorities, his invaluable leadership during the Himalayan crossing and his skillful navigation of a ship across the Pacific, which was in fact anything but pacific.

And that's the story of Penny and Polo's Sandwich Expedition and how the would-be Hamburger Crisis of 1890 was narrowly averted.

{Fig. 13 The shiny - oh so delightfully shiny culinary medal of honor!}

WHAT HO, FELLOW DAREDEVILS!

I have a smashing IDEA! If you wish to
embark upon a bold culinary adventure of your own. Get your
friends and family together, head for the kitchen and create a
superior sandwich. Then send your grand recipe to:

pennyandpolo@smackachunk.com
and receive an authentic
honorary certificate.!

TALLY HO!!!

{Fig. 14 An example of bravery - and sarcasm}

PENNY AND POLO ADVENTURES!

Penny and Polo's adventures do not end here. Why, the Pennyworths and fellow Polos have been recording their adventures since time began (penguin time that is)! They now share their ancestors' travel logs and mishaps and invite you to join them on their journeys. Go on-line and explore exciting places, meet interesting people and help them get to the bottom of all the conundrums that pop up along the way.

Why not send the chaps an e-mail? Check out their website to find out more.

www.pennyandpolo.com

About Smackachunk! and Sandwich Expedition 1890

Smackachunk! is a company where creativity rules. This creativity provides safe family fun in the form of books, audio, interactive games, on-line activities and a whole lot more. To us the story and the characters will always take center stage. We believe that a good story and high quality characters will always captivate an audience and transcend geographical and cultural borders. The Smackachunk! team aims to create high quality entertainment that encourages exploration, adventure, curiosity and learning through humor and good clean fun that kids of all ages will enjoy.

One day, while marching around the vast wastelands of Jay J. Sopp's grey matter, Penny and Polo concluded that there was nothing there to be found. Demanding to be let out, they made a bargain with Jay. They would tell him about the Pennyworth Journals, and he could illustrate them. In return, they could run amuck, adventuring once again in the human world. A deal was struck. The illustrations in Sandwich Expedition 1890 were lovingly hand painted in gouache. The painting took place in Jay's studio which measures an ample 12 square feet (it's actually a closet, but don't tell Jay). Jay's illustrations built a solid foundation for the text portion of Sandwich Expedition 1890. The first draft of the text was created by Ken Cursoe, a talented comic writer and creator of "Tiny Sepuku" from Seattle. The text was later lovingly massaged, added to and edited by Jay's wife and penguin enthusiast, Ann Halvorsen.

Be sure to check out our other great
characters @

www.smackachunk.com